CREATED BY
It's Raining Elephants

MARTHA & ME

Thames & Hudson

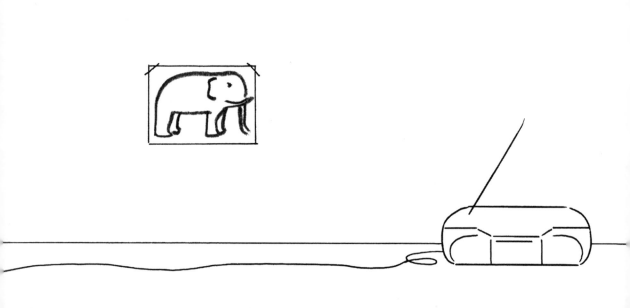

Drawing is what Martha loves most of all.

Her pictures of animals cover the wall.

All sorts of creatures, from a whale to a flea.

DAD

Then one day she paints a huge picture of me!

I step through the painting, as if it's a door

And then Martha shows me her very best roar.

I promise to stay just as quiet as a mouse

And follow her faithfully all through the house.

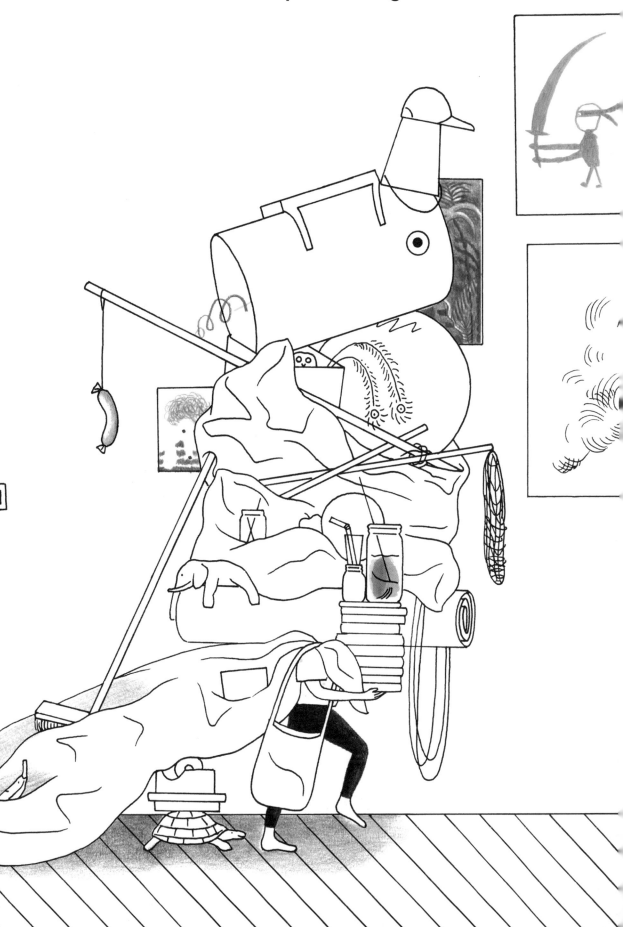

"I'm hungry now, Martha!
Is there something to munch?"

Martha growls loudly and starts to cook lunch.

While Martha is making me good things to eat,

I sneak up behind her and tickle her feet.

While I'm eating, she uses my tail as a brush...

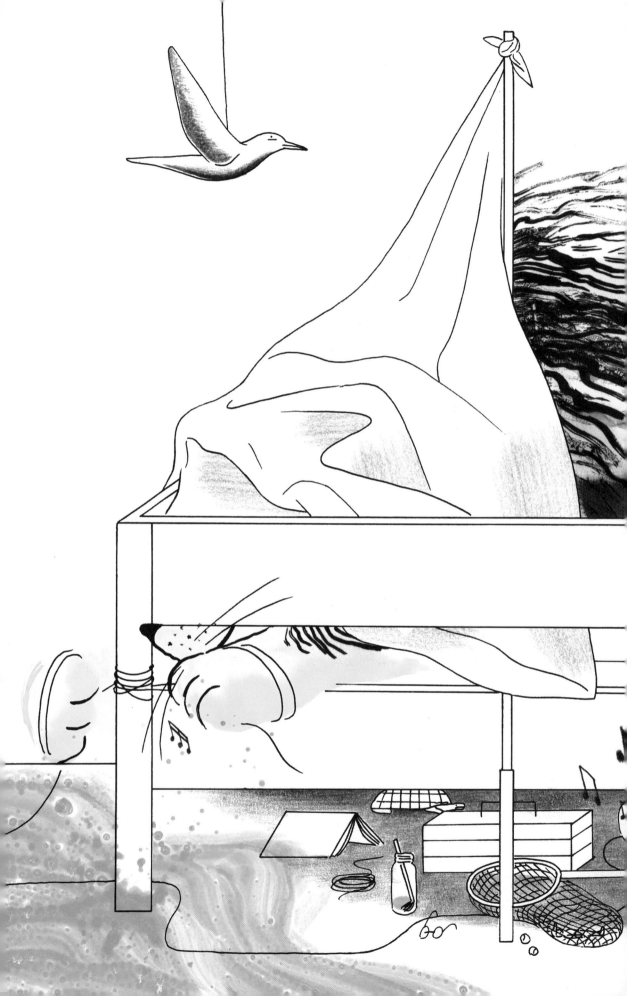

I hear the waves breaking and feel the wind's rush.

The floor is the sea and the bed is a boat!

Then the waters grow calm, and I snooze as we float.

"Hey, look! There's an island!"
are Martha's next words.

She finds a rare frog
and I chase lots of birds.

We play hide-and-seek in the jungle – what fun!

Then it's time for a water fight.
Run, Martha, run!

We splash and spray water all over the place,

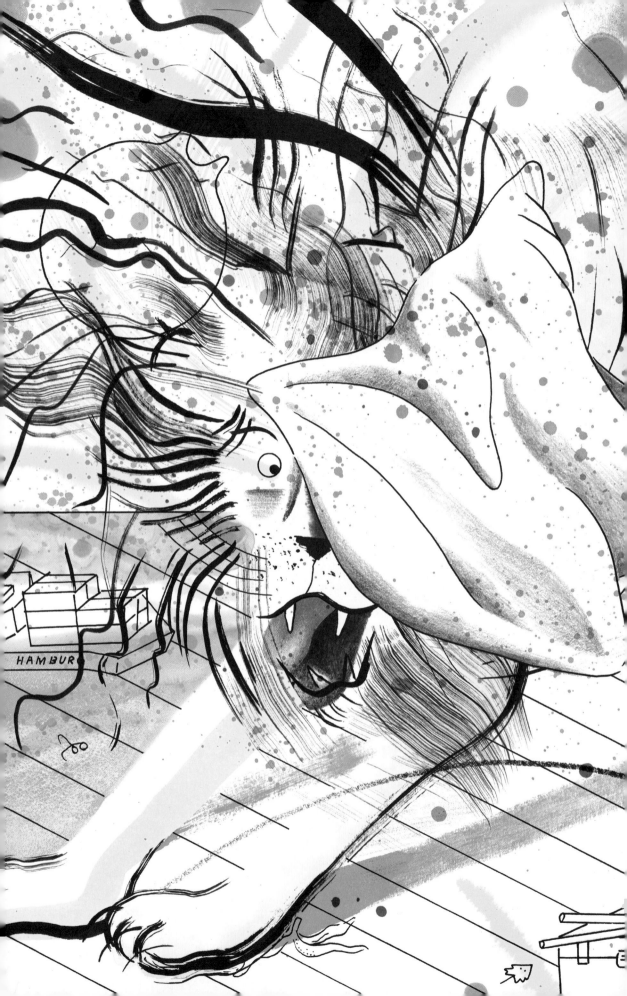

We leap and we lurk and we rush and we race.

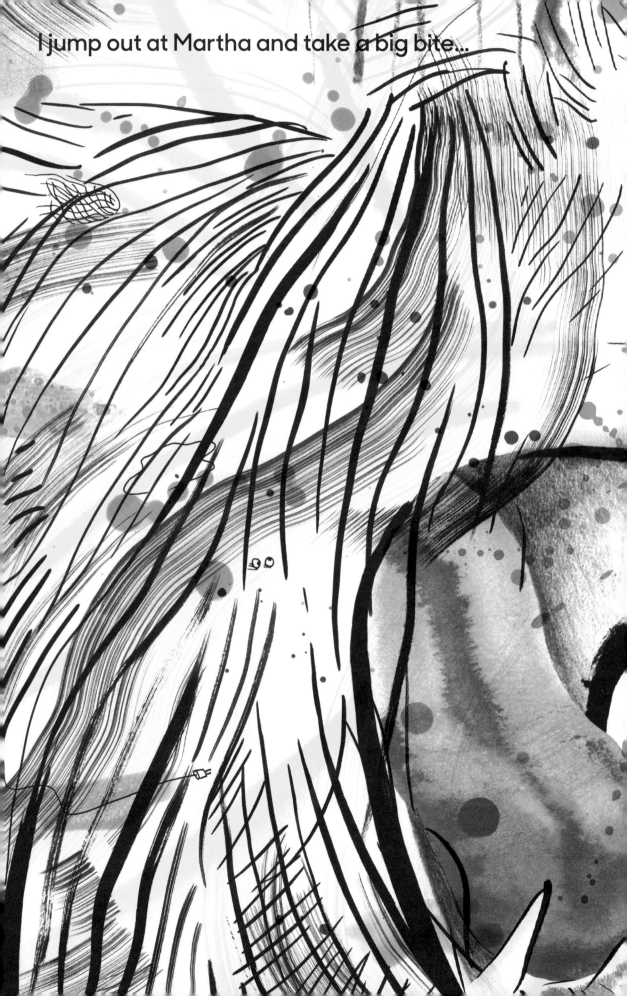

I jump out at Martha and take a big bite...

But I'm only playing! She must know that, right?

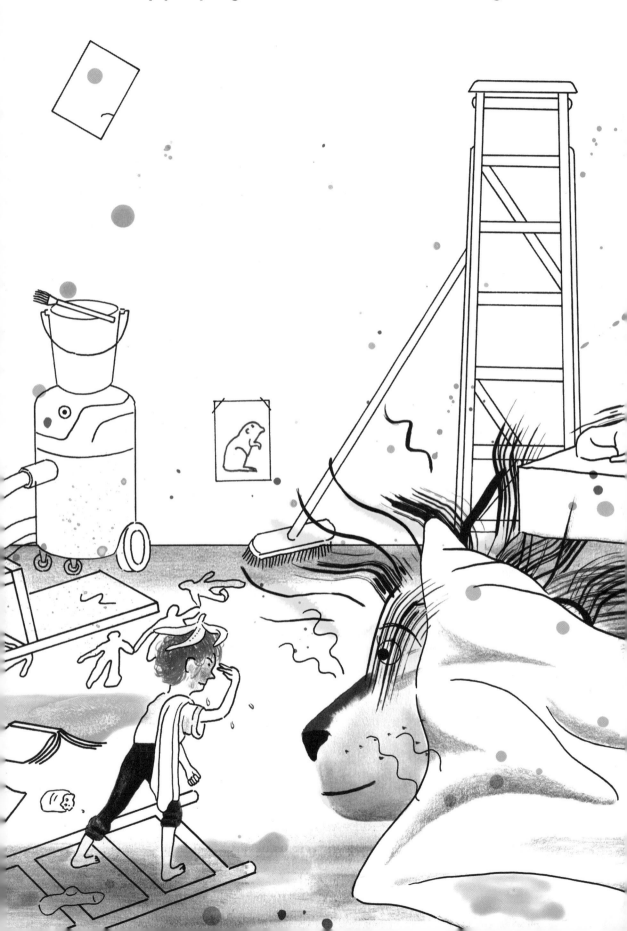

Oh no! Martha's angry! Just hear that huge roar!

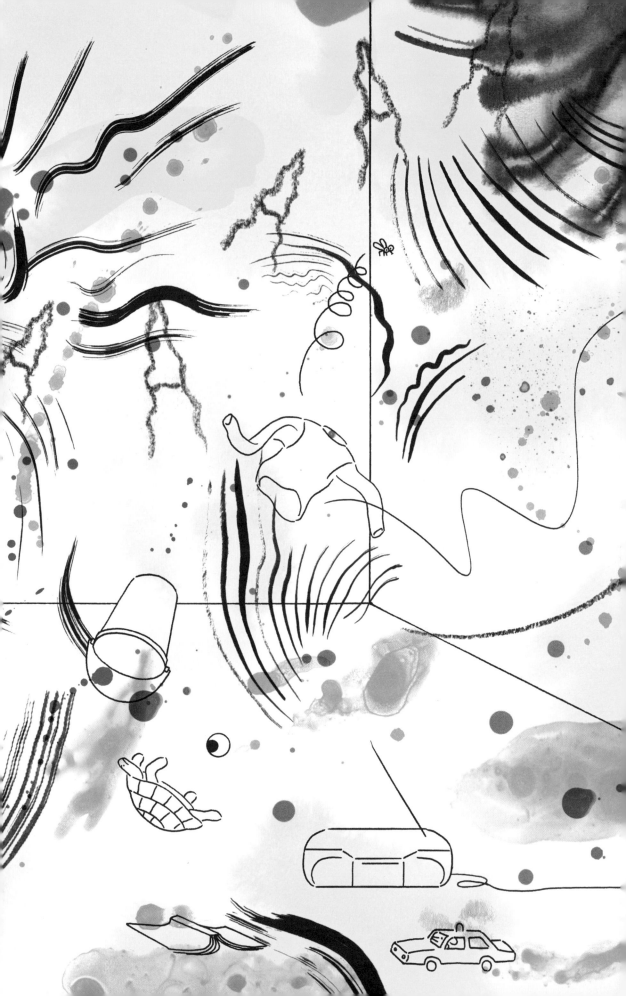

So I stay very quiet while she cleans up the floor.

My tummy starts rumbling as she lies on my back

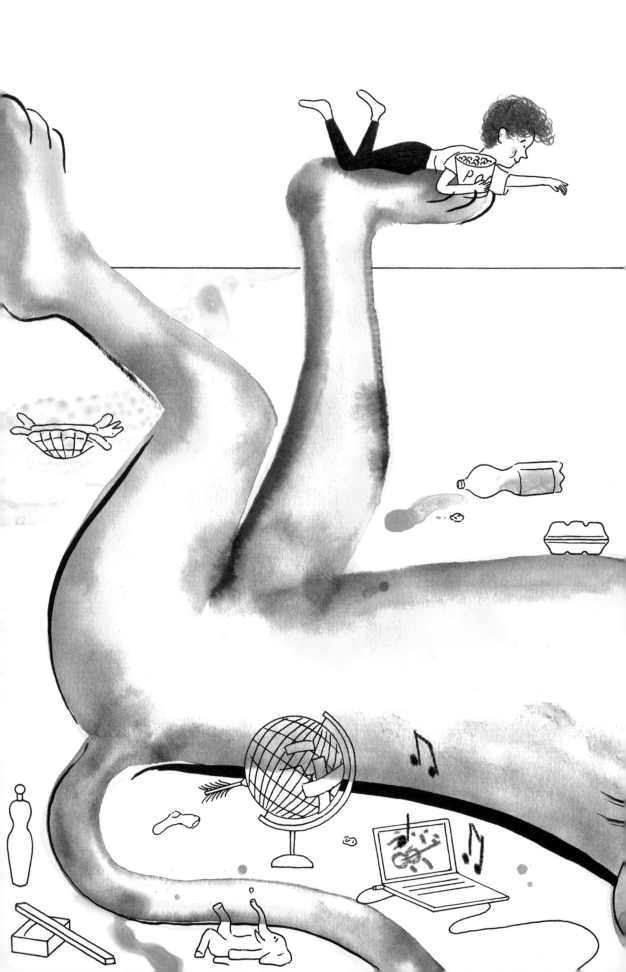

So we make friends again and she feeds me a snack.

The radio plays as we dance, sing and shout

Then we climb through a window – it's time to go out!

I don't like this cab ride, it's smelly and dark.

But it's great fun to run in the sun in the park!

I think of my home as I leap way up high

And leaving the Earth, I soar into the sky...

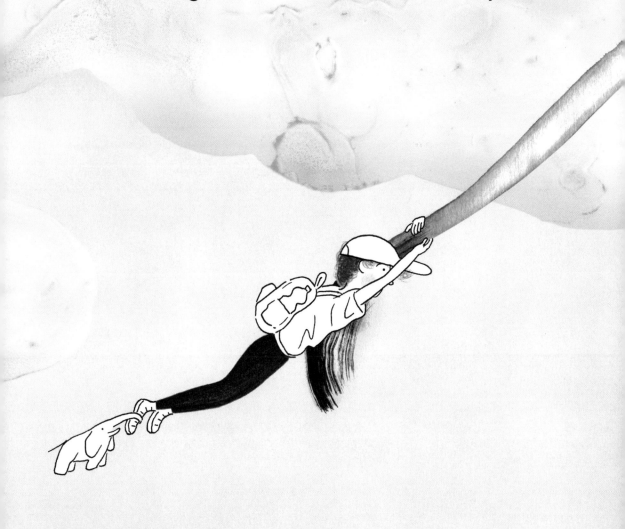

But what about Martha?
Will she be okay?

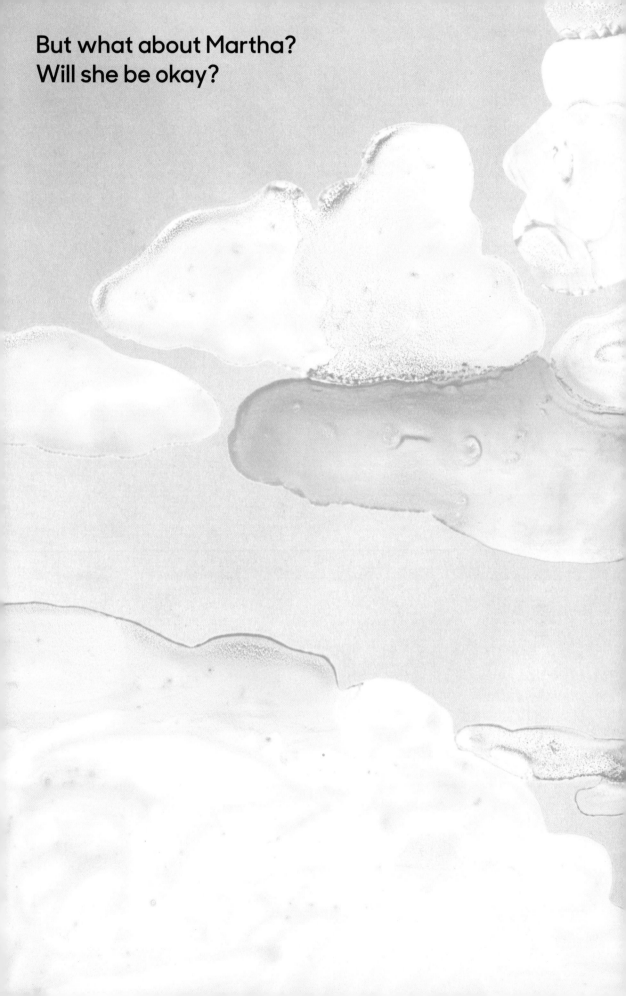

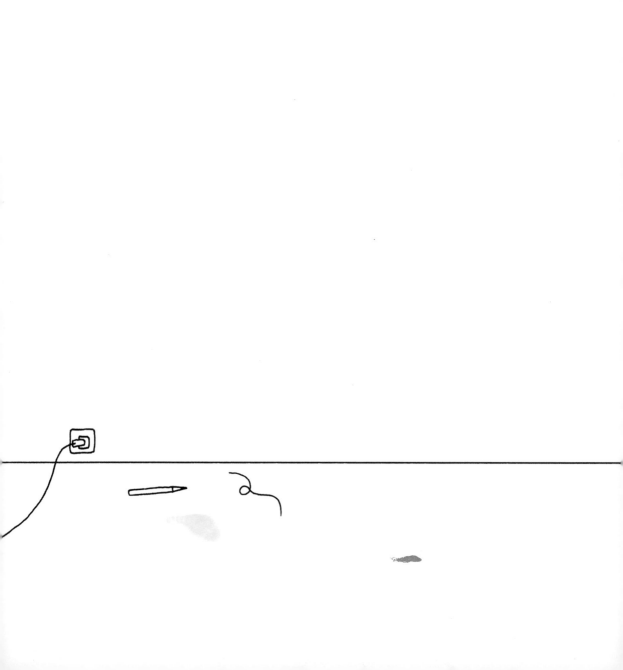

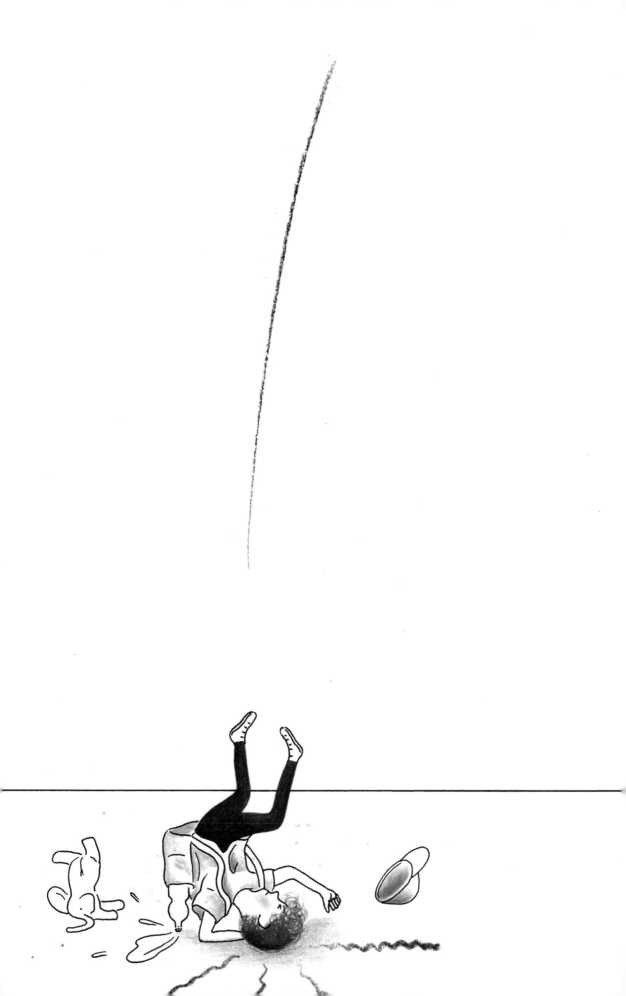

PLEASE
COME BACK

She's safe back at home, and still dreaming all day.

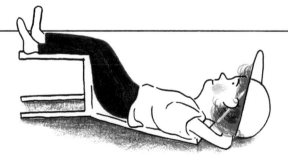

But she made me a gift.

Can you guess what she sent?

A sketchbook, a cake, and a pencil – hooray!
I really must go back to visit one day...

Text and illustrations:
Nina Wehrle and Evelyne Laube
It's Raining Elephants

Graphic design:
André Meier and Franziska Kolb

Thanks to:
Alice, Anke, Arne,
Bernd, Bettina, Birgit,
Charles,
Ellen, Evelyne,
Jeroen, Jul, Jutta,
Kathrin, Katharina, Karin,
Laura, Luca,
Matthias,
Paola,
Robi and Yolanda.

First published in the United Kingdom in 2017 by
Thames & Hudson Ltd, 181A High Holborn, London WC1V 7QX

www.thamesandhudson.com

First published in 2017 in the United States of America by
Thames & Hudson Inc., 500 Fifth Avenue, New York, New York 10110

www.thamesandhudsonusa.com

Original edition © 2017 Editions Notari, Geneva
This edition © 2017 Thames & Hudson Ltd, London

Published in agreement with Phileas Fogg Agency

British Library Cataloguing-in-Publication Data
A catalogue record for this book is available from the British Library

Library of Congress Control Number 2017938104

ISBN: 978-0-500-65142-1

Printed in China

for Cristóbal León